A
FICTIONAL
TALE OF
THINGS

by

Gary Llama

FICTION

ISBN: 978-0-9864489-4-2

Revision 2

Edited by Mo Karnage

OVOLR! / Debackle

Richmond, Virginia

USA

For

Megan and Madison

Chapter 1

I have these dreams. The kind you wake from to find yourself bathed in sweat, and still reacting to what the brain theater had chosen to show this evening. My therapist said to keep a record of them, so this is that. But this record also turned into writing about my days at work, my marriage, my co-workers, and anything else I have wanted to explore. Exploring is good. With my life the way it is now, I don't have time to explore anymore; the way she and I used to. So it's with words that I become an explorer, and shine a light on to the depths of what may seem mediocre, but is, to an extent, slowly killing me.

When I was a kid, I wanted to be a pilot. So tonight, we are flying.

Dream:

I punched through the clouds like a thread through cloth, dragging behind me the debris of flares and chaff. My ride had been locked on to. Somewhere in the desert below was an angry

Russian-manufactured missile, hunting me down like an angry 4 year-old hunts down a piñata. As a pilot, you either go higher or lower in these situations, depending on the missile and it's speed and capability, versus those of the target, which is, in this case, my jet. I have to go lower. Much lower. Down to just a few feet off the ground. They call this type of flight 'terrain mapping', or 'nap of the earth'. See, the mountains of Afghanistan prove too difficult for the navigation of slow 70s-era Russian anti-aircraft missiles. So my hope is my actions will collide the missile, following a few feet above or below my jet, with a mountain. And the hope is to do this maneuveur without crashing the jet. Sometimes the mountains prove too difficult for both missiles and jets. But tonight we are taking that risk.

I'm dropping altitude and scanning for the approaching missile. My aircraft's altimeter winding away like a mad man winding his watch. Scanning the dark nothing below for something that looks like a firefly, with a slight trail behind it. Port side of the aircraft I see the missle. I roll my jet into it, and drop altitude quicker, harder. This is not working as expected. This 'firefly', this missile, is so close it is illuminating my canopy.

And then it stops. Time appears to stop. If time is moving it's too slow to tell, but I'm looking up through the aircraft's canopy at what seems to be an anti-aircraft missile, suspended, just a few inches from the glass. I'm glaring at it. And behind the dark sensor glass of its nose cone, I fucking swear it's glaring at me. Like an eye. Seconds pass. I begin to notice my cockpit is now fully illuminated in amber by the fiery trail of this weapon, as if god had turned on an overhead light in the sky. A dim light. But it's really fucking beautiful. 'Why has time stopped? Am I dead?' I wonder to myself. More seconds pass. My seat and feet are drenched in sweat. 'Will I sit here forever? Should I eject? If I pull the handle will time start again?' My mind runs through these questions a few times.

My eyes were beginning to fatigue from the dim light, passing in and out of complete darkness. I squint and stretch them to compensate. Peering into the smoky glass of the nose of this projectile, I begin to see a light emerging. Dim, flickering, with a bit of a glow. The projectile is arming itself.

Fridays are a motherfucker. Weekend, but you still have to go in to work. My coworkers don't seem to acknowledge this tragedy and spend most of the day excited. How the fuck are they excited? My therapist says I have a negative outlook, but I always tell her its realistic, to which she forces half of her mouth into a smile, her face not escaping the look of concern she held seconds earlier, and holds through most of our sessions.

She's a nice lady. What a job though. All those people coming to your house. I wonder how she copes with that? How many times do folks freak out and show up there? I always notice the clientele as I arrive and they leave. It's always a mid to late forties person coming out to some kind of fourty thousand dollar car, like a Saab or a BMW. Just nice enough to justify working their whole life away without killing themselves, but not nice enough to actually be worth it. I imagine their problems, and how they tell them to her. "If this keeps up I may have to dip into savings!" I picture a middle age man telling her, holding his head as if cupping a headache that he's had since he moved out of the city eighteen years ago. A headache made up of trips to Lowes to fix things he doesn't give a shit about, like that light at the end of his driveway that burnt out last summer that he either has to fix or admit defeat to. I really don't know how she deals with it.

But right, back to talking about work. If you can't tell, I'm not getting anything done today. Telling stories of the folks that come to my therapist's office probably indicates to you that I have nothing better to do. My boss, and his boss would disagree. I have so many things to do. But I just can't do them yet. Work, this early might scar whatever little hope I have left for life. So I'm taking it easy, making a list to tackle, and over the next 20 minutes will slip into that list; like a cool rain that will hold me just enough unconscious until it's time to surface for lunch, then hopefully, submerge again until 4:30.

Most of these folks cope with coffee, and so mornings here smell like Starbucks. Everyone walking around so happy to be here, coffee in hand. I don't understand why you would want to be awake for this, let alone caffeinated for it. I try to minimize exertion and just plow through steadily.

I can't remember why I work here sometimes; but really it's because of my wife. She heads up the marketing for this company. And I, being a musician, and this a musical products company, seemed a "perfect fit" to her. At least, that is what she said. I suspect her idea of perfection had more to do with the facade of positivity she sometimes slathers on when faced with a situation that could result in an endless string of non-solutions, versus taking one that COULD possibly work. She's good like that. I sometimes wonder why I'm with her; her being so professional, un-movably happy, strategically planning how to succeed at almost everything. Whereas, I'm strategically planning how to just survive with the least amount of loss in my circuit; my circuit being my energy, and my life. But then I remember how the other half of her is; adventurous, daring, realistic about everything yet imaginative about anything. But you'd never guess it by seeing or talking to her.

She has a gift with marketing, and by

marketing I mean coming up with solutions that seem so obvious for a company to do, yet at the time they are introduced, seem almost absurd. And then she sells them these brilliant ideas. Every time. She's amazing.

So I work here helping to design 'musical products'. This floor is a sea of businessman, failed musicians, failed musicians turned businessman, and managers who think our six-by-nine inch paper cone shitbox of a ceiling speaker is god's gift to commercial audio. What is commercial audio, you ask? You ever heard music at the bank? That's probably our speaker. The company was started decades ago, and back then, it really did do some ground breaking stuff for audio. Which is why I decided to try working here. But, over the last few decades, the company changed hands between buyer after corporate buyer, and now, there really isn't much left of the original company other than the logo. All our stuff is made overseas, and our flagship product was designed more than twenty years ago. But our customers 'trust it'. So here I am, a lover of music helping push out a speaker system that, at best, keeps people from going postal in the post offices, or killing themselves in the banks that make up the core of our 'installation base'. Miles Davis would shit himself if he heard a muzak version of one of his tunes coming out of our fine product.

Truth be told, I wonder everyday why I'm still here. I really should think about quitting. I have friends in the weapons industries that are making a killing! I mean, if you can stomach that kind of thing. But I could imagine myself watching the news and seeing the footage of some strike in whatever war we are currently in, hearing the name of our product being used, and then wonder if my work made that possible. So when I think about the people in the banks and post offices listening to our projection of muzak; it doesn't seem that bad. A minor tragedy for the state of music, versus an actual tragedy. I wonder to myself how many of my co-workers contemplate the same thing over their lattes.

I don't belong here. None of us belong here.

Chapter 2

Dream:

I'm running. Past trees. In the woods. I know I'm being chased. I'm not sure what for, but I know my survival depends on constant movement. The men behind me wear suede trench coats. Horrible, suede trench coats. But I suppose the types of folks to chase people through the words are not going to be folks that have decent taste in clothing. Taste; its an odd concept. To assume an American has taste, puts forth in my head the idea of an American eating, which brings forth the idea of grease-filled fast food, sipping a beverage from a straw like a four year-old, and dressed accordingly, in a mash up of Walmart bargain bin stonewash and matching denim shirt. Their ass, adhered like lacquer to the leather of their oversized American car. Heart attack seconds away, like the push of their OnStar button.
Running.

Right. I'm running through this forest and

alongside me, the ground is littered with little plastic magazines. Not magazines like Time or Fortune, but magazines like fifteen-shot nine-millimeter magazines for a handgun. I should mention I'm running with a gun. And the gun has no magazine, so I have no bullets.

The magazines covering the forest floor are made of translucent plastic, like that of a child's water gun. And between the translucence and the moonlight you can see they are all loaded, the brass of the bullets stacked up through each magazine's throat. From the couple of times I've slowed down and wildly grabbed a few of them, I've learned that not many of them will fit my gun. Perhaps none of them will. So the object of this dream is to either run from the threat of the men chasing me, indefinetly, or take a chance picking up a magazine, hoping it fits, and ending this chase right here. It's an interesting dilemma, and I know it carries some meaning. Perhaps that's why I have this dream, and stay in it for so long. I do know I'm dreaming. But I've been having this dream for so many years now, that I just stay in it hoping to see a new clue as to why. So far, I can tell you two things: 1) The men never catch me, and 2) none of these magazines ever fucking fit.

*

The first time I met my wife was at a dodge ball game. I should have realized this would either end in disaster or marriage. I had left my comfort zone to be there. Dodge ball is heresy to baseball, kind of like our muzak stereo speakers are heresy to proper music loudspeakers. On the advice of friends, I had come along to the park, one of many in my fine city, to try and play this game. A break to the monotony of the life my friends view as that of a 'shut in'. I'd call it 'decisively avoiding things I don't like' but I guess it could be viewed either way, sometimes even by me.

It had been at least a couple decades since I last played dodgeball, probably in primary school. Yet, where the games of my youth were played with awkward kids acting out the early stages of what would come to be our adult socialization, here we are, acting out a fantasy of not wanting to admit defeat to life. My cohort at this game is a group of young adults whom, despite appearances, work some pretty good jobs, and despite tattoos and seemingly unwashed hair, probably care just as much about appearance as those we sneer at driving by;   suburban bound, in their vehicles of suicide avoidance.

My wife was the one that didn't seem to fit in. You could tell she saw a certain amusement in us all standing here, being adults, yet trying to get this game going. I wondered if perhaps she was drawing the same comparisons I had about the game. But I think she was actually having fun. Later I'd learn that she was probably excited about being, statistically, on the winning team. Really, any team with her on it will be the winning team. She's good like that.

Around the end of the fourth inning I finally talked to her. The teams had taken a break from playing, and upon sitting down on a bench I saw her coming over towards me. "You don't drink?" she asked. "Naw." I replied. "Cool, I'll sit over here with you then." she said, swinging her leg over the warped wood of an old picnic table. The sun was beginning to set. The breeze came in off the river, which is about 100 yards away I'd guess, guessing because I don't really know how far a yard is, but it seems like a good guestimation.

"I haven't seen you here before." she said, smiling with a squint as the sunset pierced through the bits of her bangs hiding her eyes. "No, this is my first time." I replied, "Not at dodge ball, I played as a kid, but my first time at this park." I said apologetically. She laughed. She asked what I do, which usually means job, but unsatisfied with my reply of recording bands for a living, she asked "No, I mean what YOU do?" Interesting. She was addressing a social fauxpaux that I have always resented, yet somehow here I am, playing the role I actually despise. Dammit! "Oh, I write songs, play music." I replied. "Cool." she said. "Do you have any of it with you? I'd like to hear it. I love new music!"

I told her I had some in my car around the corner, and we could go check it out, if she really wanted to. "I'd love that." she said.

Walking over to my car, it occurs to me that there is no way she'd 'Love' to hear my music, as probably everyone on the field today was a musician, and she is most definitely overrun with friends and acquaintances trying to shove their demos down her throat; the unfortunate byproduct of having musician friends. Something else must be up, I thought. Is she a friend of Iris? Iris was my ex. She's a nice girl, but she always has some issue with something that happened in our relationship. It was a very OK relationship, but it just lacked that something. You know, that something that makes you passionately excited about a person, rather than just mildly excited about them? That thing. And so from time to time I get calls from Iris, or emails, asking about why I did a certain thing, or said a certain thing, or apologizing for how she handled a certain thing during that relationship. And occasionally its extended into friends of hers talking to me about how maybe I should say a certain thing, or apologize for a certain thing, in order for Iris to move on with her life. These situations usually start like this one. A disarming chat that leads us to the news of the actual mission this friend of hers is on. I really wish she'd could move on with it. But there really wasn't anything wrong with either of us, Iris, however, takes things way too seriously and personally. She thinks that the failure of a relationship is somehow related to something she did, when in reality, it's just an unfortunate, string of bad breaks. We've all had them. Poor Iris.

Upon getting to the car, the news of her intent is broken. "Hey, would you like to go on a date?" she asked, way too energetically. "Uh, sure?" I said, spoken like a half question. "Sure." I affirmed. "I'm sorry, you're just super cute and you seem interesting." she said both enthusiastically and apologetically. "Oh, thanks. You're cute too." I added. "Want to go right now?" she asked. "Uh, Ok. Where do you want to go?" I replied. "My house. I make great Vegan sushi." she stated, this time even more enthusiastic. If she wasn't so young and in such good physical shape, I'd swear a few more statements like those, with such INTENSE enthusiasm, may have resulted in her suffering a heart attack. "Ok, where do you live? Do you want me to follow you?" I asked. "No, my car is fine here. Just drive, I'll tell you the way." she said.

And like that we were off, my friends drinking their cheap beers, talking strategy for the fifth inning, and at some point, probably wondering where two of their players had gone off to.

Chapter 3

The first date I had with my soon-to-be wife ended about as abruptly as it started. We had finished the sushi she had made. She was in the kitchen, putting the dishes in the dishwasher, which I knew she had in her house, because she made a point of telling me about it. I had offered to help her clean up dinner, to which she replied "I have a dishwasher!"

Her house was a collection of random things, which was reflective of the contents of her mind. She had bookcases full of books on everything. I mean, everything. From artist memoirs to medical manuals, psychology to marketing. And what a marketing section. It's odd how cheesy marketing books can seem in appearance. Many would be mistaken for books from that 'for dummies' series, like 'how to fix your Honda for dummies', 'open heart surgery for dummies'. Those kinds. The marketing books always had the picture of some successful looking guy on the front, shirt cuff just slipping past the rim of a gold watch, with a title exclaiming exactly what the book promises to do, much like a late night TV commercial for something thing that you know doesn't work. Except I get the feeling these books DO work. This place seems very nice, these bookcases look expensive. She had mentioned during dinner that she worked for a marketing firm. "Really?" I had asked. "Yeah," she replied, before adding, "You don't believe me?" almost daringly. It wasn't so much I didn't believe her, but something didn't add up. This woman was twenty-five, yet her place was amazing. None of my friends had places like this. And her intellect was beyond any I had encountered before. She knew shit beyond the knowledge of many people I have known, and in a diverse range of topics that most people wouldn't consider learning about. I brought this fact to her attention, and she exlaimed "I love to learn!" But what I really wondered was, if she was really this successful, what the fuck was she doing playing dodge ball in a park at six pm on a weekday afternoon? Why wasn't she going home from work, or listening to classical music in her car on her ride home to a life in the suburbs?

She caught on to my curiosity and

somewhat abruptly called me on it. "What, I can't be successful and play dodge ball?" "No, I mean, yes, of course you can," I said. "I'm just wondering why you would want to."

"Because I love it." She replied. And it was there I was floored. Because she loved it. Wow. Here I am, with my friends, doing things because it's convenient to both social circle and our houses. Yet, Because She Loved It. That's her reason. Because she loved it.

*

It wasn't long before we ended up dating; about three days. And it wasn't long after that before we got married. Just shy of two weeks. "Why wait? Are you not sure if you really like me?" she had asked. "No, I love you. But, well..." is about all I could muster before realizing there was no reason to wait. So we got married. And it was amazing. Really amazing. And it STAYED amazing. Sure, she has her little quirks. And sure, sometimes I wonder how the fuck she can be so positive all the time. But thats really who she is. She has her down days. But that is just who she is.

Amazing. And I love her for it.

But the one thing I never took into account in all the times that I had hoped to meet the woman-of-my-dreams, was how I would react to knowing her. And here I am, with surely the perfect match for me, yet HERE I AM. I am not amazing. I am not perfect. And as I grow older, I grow even less sure of the things I may have been sure of earlier in life. Each day seems like the black-and-white world I grew up in, becomes a little more grey. The one I sung about when I was young; the 'Us vs. Them' scenarios, have transformed into the 'us and them', being acted out just by me and a few of my friends. Some of us, working for the ethical corporation, or at least somewhat ethical company, and the THEM working for the weapons manufacturer that pays well. And at the end of the day, both of the groups come home from a job, with the day spent making shit that they believe makes the world a worse place. Some through the death of passion and spirit by boredom, and the others through physical death. Yet the guys at the weapons manufacturers actually seem happier. How the fuck could that be?

Shouldn't they be the ones having nightmares? Shouldn't they be the ones contemplating the fuck out of their actions and effects on the world? I really don't know if they do or don't, because ever since they all started working there, they never, ever, talk about it. Not like they avoid it, but they just never talk about it in any depth, like 'hey man, here's what working for a weapon's manufacturer is like', though they do talk about the specifics, like some new type of technical problem they were facing, but it's so abstract, like 'I was working on this new xyz computer chip, and the interface, well let me tell you, it kept shorting out the circuit board!' General stuff like that. Not mentioning that the circuit board shorted out and so now it won't kill people effectively, or it shorted out so it might kill the air crews loading it onto planes. Its always very abstract. For a while I wondered if I should boycott our friendship in actual protest, as my friendship, all of our friendships, probably enable them to build these things and perhaps, easier for them to not question the ethics of it all, but then that seemed like a really shitty thing to do. I still don't know what I really think about that idea.

These are the things I think about. This is 'what I do' these days. Think about how my friendships may influence the death of others, or how my own work may disenfranchise the public of their enjoyment of music, leaving enjoyment of music in public places to be provided only privately, in those times when they choose to disengage into their own personal realm of social avoidance, mp3 player in hand.

And this is who my wife has to deal with. She says she loves me. Loves the way I think. But I can tell she doesn't actually love the way I think. Partly, because she sometimes encourages me to look past the way I think in order to accomplish something. Like the job I have now. No way would I have signed up for that willingly. But she said "You could give it a try!" in an overly enthusiastic tone. I'm not criticizing her. I love that tone. If anything, her enthusiasm is the only thing that seems to break the monotony of a world seemingly devoid of enthusiasm or passion for life itself.

Leaving my soon-to-be-wife's apartment the night of our first date, I realized two things. One, I had met an amazing woman, and Two, that at some level, I may think of my friends and myself at something of a lower level when compared to someone like her. But why? Why would I think that? Am I buying in to all the crap they say about success and money and actually judging us as lower in status for not having such things? Or is it something else entirely. I didn't really know.

God, I wonder what she would say if I quit my job?

Chapter 4

Dream:

I'm stepping through bushes. The ground is wet. Soaked. I'm soaked. I'm deep in a forest and up ahead, I can see the light of what seems to be a clearing. Gunfire erupts. Dirt hits my face from passing shells. I taste the dirt in my mouth as I duck behind a fallen tree. My cohorts are army men, but unlike me, they are standing, shooting; returning fire. Their faces wrinkled with the expression of screams. They are screaming. "GET THE FUCK UP!"

I jump to my feet, moving from a fallen tree to another tree up ahead. I'm firing my weapon. I'm working like a machine. The machine, a squad of infantry men advancing on a village. We hear a jet pass by overhead, and the clearing, now visible as a place covered in houses, erupts in flames. The soldiers erupt in joy.

We assemble by a ravine, on the other side of the village, inspecting the bodies of those who tried to flee. They look Asian. They are Asian. They are Vietnamese. I'm in Vietnam...

What the fuck am I doing in Vietnam? It's 2014 and I'm having a dream about Vietnam? The squad assures me that this is not a dream. I disagree, and tell them I am dreaming, and that I'm too young to have been here, but they disagree. I wake up, covered in sweat, and sweating through my sheets. Am I sick? Why am I so damn hot? The bedroom is warm. The previous night was nine degrees Fahrenheit. Tonight it must be warmer, but the heater didn't get the message. I throw my blankets off. If I am sick, it usually starts out like this; complex dreams and sweating. When I was young, I had a horrible dream of being stuck in the attic with my dad, being told I had to calculate the square footage of the attic space so that we could lay down the right amount of insulation. The kind of insulation with the pink panther cartoon character on it. Do they still make that? Did they get a trademark for it? Do I have to have trademark permission to mention it now? I look over at my wife. She's fast asleep. A deep sleep. The corners of her mouth curling into a smile. Even asleep, she's so fucking positive.

Breakfast that morning was the usual affair; her with eggs and me with toast and cereal. I contemplate asking her what we would do if I quit my job. I think she'd ask me why, then accept whatever reason I gave. I'm not working for the money. The real reason I took that job was to just get out of the house. To do something. To have purpose again. There is just something about working for someone else that makes things more real. I needed that. Having spent the abundance of my life self-employed, and usually working from home, or a home-like setting, a person's reality begins to blur together. Days begin to blur together. The instances of interaction with new people become just a hologram projected in my home, as if they are not really here. The money is real. The stress is real. Maybe it's just that I don't suffer enough. Maybe I equate suffering with meaning, or reality. Anyhow, I don't work for the money; we are fine with money. But going to work was my attempt to socialize, or assimilate into something; To feel real. So before I can quit, I need to make sure it's for the right reasons, and not just an attempt by to give up and retreat into what is comfortable. After all, I hated working for myself.

Years before, I had run a recording studio. Well, I had run a mastering studio, and freelanced on the recording side of things. Mastering, to those unfamiliar, is the final process in recording. You put the finishing touches on recordings. In modern terms and practice, we basically make the recording loud as shit, but a real engineer would never admit that. It would be like Playboy admitting they are a porn magazine and not a magazine for 'sophisticated gentleman'. But that doesn't stop us from making the loudest records possible, just as much as it doesn't stop teenagers from jerking off to Playboy.

The work wasn't bad, and I was pretty good at it. What sucked was the clients. I should rephrase that; What sucked was SOME of the clients. Ninety-nine percent of the clients were awesome, but one percent made you question why you do anything. Bands that just wanted to get signed. That's all they would talk about. "Can you get us signed?" they'd ask, as if since I can make a recording, I can get people to financially back their project. It wasn't their lust for money, or fame, that disgusted me. It was the comparative experience between my own behavior at their age, and theirs. When I was in their situation, all we gave a shit about was making the music and sharing it. And so with these kids, I saw a deadening of the culture, the culture of punk rock, dwindling from that of a rich culture of social change and agitation to something where punk was just a genre. And it infuriated me.

I think it also hurt, because in the time I had been engineering, I had slacked off on making my own music. And so here I was, making the 'sign me' kids' records louder than a jackhammer, while the sounds of my own music were left as bits of loose thought floating around my head, hoping to one day get strung together into a song. And those sounds grew less articulated with each day. Pretty soon the potential songs in my head had banded together into a dull drone, and were pressing themselves into the part of the brain that causes sickness and depression. And so sickness and depression followed.

The day I closed my studio down was

bittersweet; I was sad for the craft I left behind, yet i was happy that the songs in my head would finally be free.

In the studio experience, I learned that I do not like working for myself. I do not like having to find clients, or do the money side and pay the rent and worry on how to market my business. I hated all of that. And so, like an idiot, I went into a new industry as self-employed. It was a horrible experience as well.

So that is why I'm making 'musical products'. That is why I put on this stupid tie that is choking me, this stupidly stiff shirt, and try not to piss all over the front of my pants when I'm in the bathroom before I run out the door to work each morning. Because in this job, I receive the external validation that my therapist says I probably need. Sometimes I judge this tradeoff as selfish, selling shit speakers to the world so I can feel like my life is real. Sometimes I beat myself up about it. Because, while I know I need to take care of myself, deep down, I know that my worry of being selfish is actually true.

So quitting requires me to find out if this is

a case of having the wrong job for me, or if I'm sabotaging myself into self-employment, or worse, no employment. I really do not want my wife, to come home so happy, and see me, clad in yesterday's clothes, doing nothing, and steadily growing a hate for everything around me. That would destroy any ability I have to rationalize how her and I are together.

With that thought, I finish my cereal, kiss her on the cheek, and walk out to the car.

So begins another day.

Chapter 5

"Age?" the doctor asked. "Twenty Five." I replied. The doctor's office was nice. It had been a while since I had been in one, especially one this nice. I had been without insurance for a while, but luckily, I was able to find a doctor I could afford out-of-pocket. The magazine rack had rows of magazines, carefully aligned next to each other. 'Golfers weekly', the cover said. There was another golf magazine as well. 'What is it with doctors' offices and golf?' I thought to myself. Do they think their patients are just running in here between time on the course to get a checkup, and maybe work on a handicap while waiting?

"You know your tooth is rotting," the doctor said, before adding, "I can see it from all the way across the room." Wow. A shiver runs up my spine and bursts into a sadness that settles across my body. "Yeah… I don't have the money to get it fixed." I replied. "You should get that fixed, it's rotting out of your head." she said. 'Yeah, I wonder why that didn't occur to me before now?!' i think to myself, but just reply with a nod.

"So why are you here today?" she asked, now seemingly annoyed. I start to explain the issue. "I have this sore, on my backside, well, my buttock, and at first I thought it was a pimple, but now I'm not sure. It's really big. I had something similar to this a year ago, but I thought that was a onetime thing." The one before this, well, it was an eye opener. I had driven twelve hours non-stop back from the holidays. Before I had left, I had bought some slim fitting jeans, and a couple days later, the area that I had been sitting on had become sore. Fast forward a few days and it's like a boil. A few days after that, it had become even bigger. What had started out like a golf ball had now becoming something like a softball. I had no insurance, and no clue what to do. Finally, I drove to the ER in desperation. The drive was quite a debacle of balancing my weight on my heels to keep my rear off the seat and ease the already excruciating pain. Driving down streets I had driven for years, I learned every bump with painful exclamation. At the ER, I was shepherded into the inflow of awaiting patients at the city hospital. A woman in the corner, waiting longer than I had been, would vomit every few minutes into a bag she held close to her face. "They don't care about us." I thought. I longed for the pediatrician I saw as a kid who took every cough and sneeze as something to be dealt with in a timely fashion. After waiting for a few hours, they took me back to the rooms, but as I pulled down my jeans to show the wound to the nurse, I noticed a dripping. The wound had opened. A surgical team and some morphine later, they released me, high on morphine, to drive myself home.

This doctor, however, didn't feel the need for surgery that previous doctors had shared. "Yeah, that's pretty big. Have you been tested for MRSA?" she asked. "Yes," I replied, "these seem to occur with no infection of any kind." I said. "Well, let's treat you for MRSA, just in case." she said, stubbornly. And so she wrote the prescription, and sent me on my way, reminding me again to fix my tooth. Painfully, I get back in my car and drive home.

*

My wife was my saving grace with this

condition. Unlike the years before where I would have to drive myself everywhere when infected and in pain, she held the line of humanity and was always nearby to remind doctors that exerting the minimum effort on their part, will not be tolerated. Before I met her, I had been scared that I may never find a partner who would accept me in this physical condition. Who wants a man with such issues? It is not sexy. And it isn't attractive. So, for a few years, I isolated myself from dating, feeling sickly, diseased, and broken. But those fears had underestimated the kindness a person could have in their heart. My wife was such a person.

"How is work going?" my wife asked. It's dinner time. We are seated in our kitchen. For some reason we eat here, even though I think we'd both be more comfortable on the couch. It's a thing she does to add 'structure'. And, it works. What would mostly be spent as time with us each drifting off, facing away from one another, here we are forced to communicate. To be human. To be intimate. "It's going ok," I reply. "we just redesigned the enclosure for the JA9000, our main auditorium speaker, to make it more resistant to impact." I say. "Nice!" she replies, smiling, engaging me fully with her eyes. "How is your work going?" I ask her. "Oh, it's good. That client we had been trying to get, you know the hospital chain; we got them. You should have seen the look on their faces when we pitched them the project! Total disbelief..." She continued. "And they ended up going with us! I think they could tell that their current system wasn't working and they needed to trust us to deliver. So they agreed to trust us." After a quick pause, she added 'So that means this year, we can take some time down at Oceancrest." "Nice!" I replied. Nice.

Oceancrest is a bubble of happiness. Actually, it's an old town bordered by farms and the Atlantic. We have a house there. We used to rent it out during the off-season, then during the on-season, but after a while we decided that playing maid to the exploits of renters wasn't worth the money it brought in for us. So we fixed it up as our own. It didn't cost us much to get down there, just gas, but my wife sometimes couldn't afford the time off from work to meet the goals her firm wanted her to achieve for the year. This hospital deal put them into the black, early. So we could count a few weeks of slow living, disconnected from everything that seems to steal our attention, and just focus on enjoying the moments together. My dream would be to move there permanently, but with her job, we need to be closer than Oceancrest would allow. And vacation loses its charm if you're telecommuting the entire time. I think what I love most about the place is how WE are when we are there, rather than anything special about it, itself. 'Hell, this time, we might even be able to stay a month or so!' I thought to myself.

My wife gets up from the table, and puts her dishes in the sink, before moving off towards the living room. I take my dishes over and put them on top of hers, and begin scraping the remnants of dinner down the garbage disposal. I hit the switch and the disposal cranks to life. "Brdgrdgrdgrdgr" it said. I rinse the dishes clean, and one by one stack them into the dishwasher. The dishwasher! I remember when this was one of the things I looked forward to having in life. I used to hand wash everything. I remember I'd let myself own no more than three or four utensils so as to avoid an apocalyptic buildup of dirty dishes that would inevitably need to be tackled some day.

I load the soap and shut the door, then move on towards the living room. "Pick out something to watch!" my wife says enthusiastically. "What about this?" I ask, highlighting a movie on the television menu. "Hm, pick something else!" she says, excitedly. We find a movie and begin watching, my brain unwinding from the earlier day at work. Her brain... well I have no idea what her brain does, but it must recharge at some point.

Chapter 6

"Hey Buddy!" my boss, John says, shaking my hand enthusiastically. "Come in and take a seat." I follow him into his office. The office looks like half of a kid's bedroom, and the other half torn out of a bohemian loft. I take a seat in one of the two heavy recliners he has sitting in front of his desk. Everything in here is beefy, unlike most office furniture. The tables are huge, built sturdy, products of an era where things were built to last. John is much the same way. His large voice ripples through the walls, filled with the joy that he holds for his job and this company. He's one of the old guys. He's been here since the days when the company was making studio speakers; the same speakers that inspired a golden-age of artists in studios across the country, Those products shaped the sound of blues, R&B, and top forty in the sixties and seventies. It's kind of amazing to think about. Behind his desk, he has one of the original audio systems set up; a vacuum tube amplifier and turntable, set on a large credenza. On the walls are his guitars; well-worn classics that I imagine him taking down and strumming throughout the day to break the monotony.

"We just love your wife's work," John says. "She has done a LOT for this company! When we heard she had a husband who was in the industry, it was a no brainer to hire you!" I laugh. "Thanks, John." I say. He leans forward. "So how are things going?" he asks. Then continues, "I've been looking over your work and you've been doing an amazing job! The redesign you did for the 9000 series enclosure was spot-on! We've been trying to get something better for 10 years, and you just came in and nailed it!" John says, his smiling eyes piercing through me. This is weird. He is so excited about our work, and I, apparently am helping it along, yet cannot stand it. Can he tell? Can he sense that I hate this job? A record cover in the corner of my office catches my eye. The Beatles. Fuck. Why does everyone in this industry love the fucking Beatles so much? It's not that I hate the Beatles, but I hate what people make the Beatles out to be. At best, they were a boy band, a 60's equivalent of that group Justin Timberlake used to sing for. But folks treat them as the inventors of all rock n roll. Which is borderline racist. No, it's actually fucking racist. Blacks in the south created rock n roll. Elvis stole the sound. The Beatles turned it into money. They were good at turning music into money, I'll give them that. They pioneered that. I guess it's kind of fitting to see that LP hangin here. After all, were doing the same thing to sound nowadays. Turning it into money, with little appreciable advancement, or betterment, or respect for, what came before. But John was from the early company. He worked on the products that built this company's name. I wonder how he feels going from helping Motown shape American culture, to keeping the post office filled with muzak.

"Are you Ok?" John asks. "Oh, Yeah, I was just thinking. You've been here a while, right?" I ask as nicely as possible. "Yes Sir, since our third year! It was an amazing time, we built the old Mk 1," he says motioning to the speakers behind him. "We changed the industry!" I nod my head smiling. "So how are you getting on?" John asks, in a more serious tone. "Well, I'm getting on,' I say.. 'acclimating myself to the product line still, but

I'm learning it." I respond, completely hiding my dislike for both the product line and the job. "Great!" John says.. 'Look,' he says, "the reason I called you in today, well, besides checking in to see how you are doing with the job, is corporate has decided to move some folks around to work on a new product..." He pauses, looking up at the drop ceiling of his office. "...they asked me to lead the project. Told me to pick a team..." John takes a pause, leans back and says, bluntly. "...I want you on that team." I pause for a second, trying to collect myself and figure out what I may be agreeing to. "Oh, yeah, Ok, what are we building?" I ask, somewhat surprised by the thought of a change in the job I hate. "Well, I gotta ask you a few questions." he says, grabbing a stack of papers from a folder hidden under even more papers laying on his desk. I realize his desk is actually kind of a mess. He puts his glasses on, and clicks on a lamp in front of him. It's already bright in here, the sun blaring in the windows lining his office. My eyes adjust. "Have you ever been convicted of a felony? I know we asked this on the entrance exam for the job, but we gotta be on the level for this, so

I have to ask." he says in a serious tone. 'Felony? Well, yeah,' I think to myself. '...but I was found not guilty on appeal. So I guess that counts as a no'. "No." I reply. "Good, Good." John replies, scanning the sheet. "Have you ever been committed to an institution or held for mental observation?" he asks, reading off the next question. 'Geez. Yeah...' I think to myself, '...but upon reconsideration, the judge deemed that the circumstances for my commitment were of a 'particular nature' and struck them from my record, so no, no I have not'. "No." I reply. "Great!" John says. "Have you, at any time worked for a foreign government?" he asks. "No" I reply. "Well, I just wanted to hear it from your mouth," John says. "We have already run your background check, but I just wanted to hear it from you. You passed, by the way. But corporate has a lot riding on this project. Every team member is under my name. My career is on the line for this. So think about what I'm going to show you today, and if you have any reservations about it, any at all, tell me now. We can't afford to move employees around once we are in the field; It would look like we don't know what we are doing." he says. "The contractor will doubt us. And it will look like I don't know what I'm doing here as the team leader. And corporate won't like that." he emphasized. I nodded my head, understanding. "Sure, sure, I understand." I said in a sympathetic tone. John smiled. Without looking, he moves his hand to his right, grabs a folder, and hands it to me. "Read this!" he says, then reclines back into his chair, his eyes peering at me through the bottom of his glasses. The folder is stamped "secret". I open it and begin reading. Odd words, diagrams; codenames? I can't believe my eyes.

"What do you think?" John asks. "Sounds good..." I reply, not looking up, still immersed in the folder's contents. "Great!" John replies, "We will leave within the week." "Leave?" I ask. "This is a field assignment," John says, "Grace already knows about it, Hell, she got us the deal!" "Oh, well, OK then!" I say. John stands up, I stand up. John leans his large frame in towards me and grabs my hand. "We are glad to have you on board." John says. "Thanks, John!" I say. We walk to the door, and I walk back out to my office.

Chapter 7

"Age?" the woman asks. "Twenty Five." I reply. The room is cold. White. Cinderblock. It's about a quarter-past midnight and I'm tired. My face feels numb. My eyes feel clogged from the tears that flowed from them earlier that night. We are sitting around a table of unusually low height, like a kindergarten classroom table. The woman looks over the forms. A deputy walks in. "Here are his personal items; clothes, ID, pack of cigarettes and lighter." the deputy says, handing her the bag of items. "We can't have cigarettes on this side." she says dismissvely. The deputy pulls the cigarettes out and tosses them into the trashcan at the edge of the room. "Have you ever thought of killing yourself before?" the woman asks. "Um, in what sense?" I ask. Of course I've thought about it. Who doesn't? If this is the test of sanity, it seems like the insane are the people who wouldn't have THOUGHT about it. "And you tried to kill yourself tonight?" she asks. "No, I was just depressed. But look, I'm fine now." I say, trying to be convincing, but with very little enthusiasm. She keeps her eyes on the forms. "Have you ever tried to harm yourself?" she asks. "No" I reply. She calls a nurse in. "Take him to level B." she says.

Now I'm in what I can only describe as a cafeteria. It's closer to nine in the morning now. A guard comes over and asks me to follow him to the bathroom. I walk in and he orders me to strip. I take my clothes off, and he inspects me for wounds. I suppose they don't take your word for anything in here. "Ok, put your clothes back on." he says. I put my clothes back on, holding my pants up with my hand, the result of my belt being taken from me hours ago. We walk back into the main room. The nurses are all crowded around one of the lunch tables, caught up in the talk show on the TV across the room. "Do I get a phone call?" I ask the nurses. They don't reply. I look around the room. My fellow inmates are scattered across the large lunchroom. A couple are faced away from the TV, staring off into space. One is leaning against the wall, rocking his head back and forth. Almost everyone is rocking their head back and forth. Between the signs of mental disability in my fellow patients, and the nonchalance of the nurses watching TV, I come to realize I may be the only patient in here who will speak today. Down the hall are the dorms, where my fellow patients sleep. I imagine which of these folks will be my roommate. "Hey! Richard! You gonna regret it if you make me come down there! Sit down, boy!" a nurse yells at one of the patients. Who she is yelling at, I'm not sure, as no one is doing anything different than they were 10 minutes ago. I scan around looking for this anarchist. I ask the nurses again, "Excuse me, ma'am, Can I make a phone call?" One looks up at me, silent for a few seconds, then says "You WILL get your phone call when it's TIME!" 'What the fuck?' I think to myself. I imagine what it's like for my fellow patients to have to deal with this every day. There is no compassion. We are distractions from the television set. Do the nurses understand that their job is to take care of us? Do they understand the TV was put here for us, and not them?

An hour or so passes. "Mr. Reid? William Reid?" a small woman calls from the door of the adjoining office. I stand up. "Yes?" I answer. "You can make your phone call now." she says. I walk into the office. "Is it local?", she asks. I realize I have no idea where we are. "Is so-and-so local?" I ask. "No." she says. "Well that's where I have to call." I answer. "Keep it short." she says. I dial the numbers. She's standing behind her desk watching me. I guess she will listen to my entire conversation. How do I tell my wife that I'm surrounded by people with serious mental conditions? That they made a mistake putting me here and are holding me in a ward full of very troubled people? The phone connects. "Hello?" my wife says. "Hey, it's Will" I say. "Will?" she says, not expecting me to be calling "What do you want?" she asks. I start to explain where I am, and what happened. She already knows. "What do you want?" she asks, pointedly. "I want you to come testify at my commitment hearing this morning. They say it's at 10 o'clock. Will you do that?" I ask. "You really want me to come testify?", she asks. "Um, yeah, they have me in here with all these people..." I say, "...and they are not well, like seriously…" I whisper, "...I don't know what the fuck is going on here but I need to be somewhere else." I add. There is a pause on the line. "...Ok, I'll be there." she says. The phone goes dead. The woman in the office is now staring at me. I wonder if she just diagnosed me with something in her head. The sign on the desk says she is a social worker. "Go back out to the living room, Mr. Reid." she says, sternly. I do as she says.

We are eventually moved to an adjoining room, this one is clearly the cafeteria. Folded lunch tables fill the room. Our group huddles together around the first few tables, taking up maybe a sixteenth of the room. "Break time. You have fifteen minutes." comes across the PA speaker. I look up to see my fellow patients walking towards a door at the back of the cafeteria. I stand up. A nurse comes over to me "Do you smoke?" she asks. "I do," I reply, "but they threw my cigarettes away." "You'll have to stay inside then." she says. This woman seems nice. She seems to actually care a little. "You're shivering!" she says. "I've been up all night. It's cold in here." I say. She walks over to the nurse's station, a room splitting this cafeteria from the previous room, which also seemed to resemble a cafeteria, minus the tables, with it's windows lined with a metal grid, and heavy gates splitting the two rooms. She comes back. "Here, put this on" she says handing me a blue jacket, like the jacket a union electrician would wear. It's nice, but oddly wide for its short length. I turn it around to see the size. The tag reads "Central State Mental Hospital". I put it on, it's warm. "Can we eat?",I ask. She looks at me and says "We are worried about feeding you, seeing as you have all those food allergies. Don't worry, your hearing is in an hour; we'll get you squared away then." she assures me, in a sympathetic tone. 'Hearing?. Jeez, what the fuck have I gotten myself into?' I think to myself.

I remember I had brought a pillow with me to the hospital. "Do you have my pillow?" I ask. "Was it in your bag of effects?" she asks. "I don't think so." I answer, thinking about the small size of that bag. Damn. That was the memory foam pillow my chiropractor had told me to get for my neck issues. Its a hundred dollars. I guess when I saw the deputies arrive with the shackles, I just got sidetracked. "Motherfucker." I say to myself.

Out the door I can see the sun. I can see a fence at the end of the yard. It looks so green. I really need a cigarette.

Chapter 8

Long and black, sits the aircraft in front of me. "Wow!" I think to myself. I've always been fascinated by aircraft, especially the black ones, the secret ones. And here I am, standing in a hangar, staring at an aircraft I had never heard of, before today. And here it is. I wonder how many billions of dollars this thing has cost, and how many lies had to be told to congress by winking generals to hide it's budget, through overpriced items they will later be taken to task for as examples of 'over spending'. "A thousand dollars for a hammer?" a senator will ask. The general will check with his D.O.D. lawyer, and reply "It's a very special hammer, Sir," the two of them, almost giggling with the game they are playing. And some of the senators will be wise to the jig, and laugh a little under their breath as their idealistic fellow senator tries to build a case against military overspending before being reeled in for other questions.

"She's a beaut', eh?" says John, standing next to me with his hand on my shoulder. "Yes, she is!" I reply, eyeing the long, slender airframe. "Let's get lunch!" John exclaims, patting my shoulder with insistence.

We pull up to the drive-through. John insisted on driving, so we're in his car. One of those SUVs designed to haul half-a-dozen kids. It's comfy, and I see why folks buy them. The road feels like minor annoyance in this thing. "Two bacon cheeseburgers, two fries!" John yells into the speaker. "What do you want to drink?" he asks me, still almost yelling. "Water is fine." I reply. I had forgotten to tell him I don't eat meat. I guess I'm having fries for lunch. How do you tell a bunch of contractors working on a spy plane that you don't eat meat? They'd probably revoke my clearance right there. But John fits in well, between his American SUV and his bacon cheeseburgers, the bosses will be looking for commies elsewhere.

We pull into a parking spot and begin eating our lunch. "So what do you think?" John asks. "It's amazing!" I say. He smiles, dipping his fries into the open face of his sandwich, scrapping mayonnaise onto the fries, then shoving a wad of them into his mouth. "Yes it is." he says, voice muffled by the mouthful of fried potatoes. "So what does our speaker do in this application? Doesn't the pilot have a headset?" I ask. John nods his head. "Do you know what PTSD is?" John asks. "Yeah, I've read about it." I say, curious as to what PTSD has to do with our speaker. "Well," John says, taking a break from the fries for a moment, "...you know how all those drone pilots were having PTSD from flying? The pentagon did some studies and realized it was because they were so far removed from the action. Something about disassociation from combat, or something like that..." he says, staring at the truck's radio. "...well, they realized all pilots were suffering from this, as they fly so high from the actual action. So in an effort to curb this, or as their directive is called 'Force Accountability', they have decided to put an indicator in these planes that allow the pilot to know when their bombs have landed; To add a sense of connection to the mission."

John shifts his focus to the cars waiting in the drive-through. "So our speaker, it plays a tone when the bomb hits?" I ask, my imagination trying to grasp for some kind of sound it could make other than the sounds of screaming people. "No, it vibrates. Like an explosion. Just a simple square wave, but more vibration than tone..." he says. "If it was just a tone, we could have done this back in the lab. The reason we are here, is we need to work with the airframe itself, to get the vibration just right. They already did tests and determined a spec that would be acceptable. Our job is to meet that spec, while minimizing interference with the avionics and other systems." John stops speaking, and begins gathering the last bit of his cheeseburger in the remnants of his ketchup-covered wrapper. "So it's a bomber?" I ask. "Oh yeah, it's a bomber!" John says, stuffing the last bit of sandwich into his mouth.

We drive back to base. When we arrive back in the hangar, John takes me up on the ladder and shows me what where we will be installing the device. Peering in the cockpit, he shows me an area that is devoid of black boxes, down by the pilot's foot. "That's what we have to work with," he says. "that space right there." he says, motioning with his oversize hands and fingers. I look at the various dials and switches around the cockpit. I look down the airframe, at the fins ominously poking out from the top of the plane. I look forward through the front glass of the cockpit, wondering what it's like for the pilot to fly this thing. High above the clouds. Pitch black night. Coming in low on the terrain, then popping up to higher altitude to make the drop. "3, 2, 1..." I imagine the pilot counting, then 'pop'. The airframe lifts a bit from the sudden loss of weight, as it's bombs drop free of the aircraft and begin their journey to target. The countdown resumes, "15, 14, 13, 12..." continuing until each bomb finds it's target, and our little speaker fills the cockpit with a chilling vibration of success. "Bzzzzzzz", target destroyed. "Bzzzzz" twenty dead. "Bzzzzzzz" women and children. "Bzzzzzz". "Bzzzzzz".

I wonder if the Pentagon really thought this through. I begin to wonder what the pilots will feel anytime their door buzzer rings.

"Let's call it a day!" John says. "We're on contractor time here, days end at 2pm!" he exclaims. "Ok, tomorrow then!" I say, stepping down off the ladder. Walking back towards the door, I stop and take one more look at the black plane. "Amazing isn't it?" John says, patting me on the shoulder. "Yeah, it's amazing." I say, somewhat despondent. He pats me on my back again and yells, "Tell Grace I said Hi!"

Chapter 9

Marketing isn't just about making people buy products, it's also about making people buy ideas. And in some cases, it's making people buy ideas as solutions to the problems they are currently facing. Sometimes its to avoid public outlash at a faulty product that killed a few kids. Other times, its to avoid future lawsuits from pilots and the families of pilots, whom suffer from PTSD, while a knowing military continues to send them into battle; despite having studies that clearly show its effects. These latter situations are handled by what are called 'Crisis Management Firms'; marketers and lawyers, bundled together to help companies overcome negative opinion. Sometimes they just fix the opinion through propaganda. Other times they actually develop product ideas to help address the issue. The latter is the current situation Grace had become involved in. And as she itsn't the type of person to simply persuade the pilots and the public that PTSD could be solved through wording, she hired a development team to work on a way to try and end the problem that has caused the issue in the first place. The issue being, the rapid disassociation that pilots seem to make from their role in the act of killing.

So they came up with the speaker box idea, and having been affiliated with the innovators of loudspeakers, the 'musical products' company I work for, she found a way to get two clients on the same team. Was it ethical? I have no idea. But when Grace speaks, people tend to listen, and then become believers. Everyone wants to believe something. No one really wants to be a skeptic. Being a skeptic is lonely. It's alienating. Grace, with her charm, her wit, her intelligence, and her abundance of positivity, lends an ease to the process of becoming a believer. You just want to believe anything she says. For me, this realization is slightly disturbing, as my questions tend to be about if she loves me. But you really want to believe her. And you really do believe her. But you know she is so good at selling, that there is a chance, just maybe, that you are being sold as well. That is where trust comes in. Trust built from outcomes of past products sold. Trust from years of faithfulness and behavior that lines up with love. So I trust her.

*

"Did you get to see the 'grey lady' yet?" she asks, putting some groceries onto the countertop of the rental house were staying at for the next few weeks. "The what?" I ask. "The Grey Lady!" she says enthusiastically, before adding "...the plane!" "Oh, yeah, yeah we saw it today." I respond. "Is that its name?" I ask. It seems like a basic name for a rather ominous plane. "Oh No..." she says, "That's just the nickname. Its still on code-word basis. They haven't applied for a designation yet. Too risky at this point."

I'm sitting at the table working on my cereal. I eat a lot of cereal these days. A few weeks ago I realized it was my favorite food, and wondered why I ate anything else. Anything else is just something I eat between cereal. So why not have cereal for every meal? That was my thinking. I'll probably become a little deficient in protein, so I pack protein bars to eat at work, and save my home meals for cereal. Good plan. Perfect plan, actually. Why don't other people do this? Sugar, carbs. Then protein. Repeat. Grace thought it was funny, especially since I don't drink milk, filling my bowl with cold water, instead. "Eww!" she'd say laughingly. I'd respond, "The milk is really just about the cold, and water is cold too!" and then encourage her to try it, to which she'd just laugh and run across the kitchen as I followed after her, giggling and spitting bits of cereal out of my mouth. Its times like those I'd remember how glad I was to have met her. Before Grace, I was married to my high school sweetheart, though I had dropped out of high school before we got together. But I was a different person then. A very different person. I didn't like that person. I like who I am now, I think. I'm way happier. But still, there is something that is sad. I wonder if that 'something' is a thing I have yet to explore in therapy, or if its a thing that is just part of me.? Depressed brain chemistry, perhaps? Or a non-acceptance of my whole self, that puts me on guard toward other things, and makes fully being me, fully impossible? I don't know. 'Need to explore that.' I note to myself.

The rental house is on the beach, about 30 minutes away from the airbase we are working at. Grace picked it out. Maybe she sensed my unhappiness with the job. Maybe that's why she helped get this project together. What if the only reason she came up with the speaker idea was to help me be less depressed. Fuck. There's no way she'd do that though, not just for that.

After dinner we took a walk down to the beach, hand in hand. The breeze coming in off the ocean seemed to wash away my tension. 'She seems happy.' I think to myself. We pick up shells and throw them back into the ocean. 'Why does she never seem to show stress?' I wonder. She's amazing. We find a pier and settle down to watch the sunset. As we're sitting, a serious look comes over her face. "Will?" she says. "What do you think about having a baby?" The question smacked me upside the head. It was out of nowhere. I mean, yeah, we're married, yeah, I'm 35, and she's 32, but now? Why now? I can barely keep myself together, getting all fucked up with these existential questions. And today, I'm working on a bomber, a frigging bomber for Christ's sake, something that will inevitable kill children, and now she wants to make one?

I look at her, and in her eyes, I see this is

something she really wants. The usually enthusiasm on her face is now gone. This is serious. The look on her face is pleading with me, in both its stillness, and its strain. In her eyes I see it too. A longing. This is what she wants. Really wants. This is what her soul wants. This is what she truly believes may be her purpose in life.

"It could be cool!" I say, encouragingly. "Really?" she asks. "But aren't you afraid we'd become boring parents? You don't think we'd just be giving up on life?" she asks, trying to reconcile the words that just came out of my mouth with the contents of every conversation I've ever had with her. "I think we'd be awesome parents. We know how to handle life." I say. She smiles and laughs a little. "I'm pregnant." she says. Wow. Kaboom! You know, when sometimes you just go a little numb, but something takes over you and you just head right into the fear, like you just poke your face right through its mesh and deliver what you need to say? This was one of those moments. It's not like we had been trying to NOT get pregnant. We'd actually been trying regularly, I suppose, though not with that aim in mind. But I guess if you practice enough, you may find yourself in the big game. This was the big game. I put my hands up to her face, holding the side of her cheek, and softly spoke the following words...

"Let's be parents."

Chapter 10

Dream:

"Do you know what sadness is, boy? Its this!" the man intones, flailing his arms together towards a set of screens on the other side of the room. The screens flick alive with the black-and-white image of a girl. Sad. Close up. Bow in her hair. Crying. "It's my daughter!" I realize. The screens go black.

"Do you know what despair is, boy?" the man says, and swings his arms behind us. Another image flicks to life. It's me. Sitting on my bed. Sad. During the years I thought I didn't have much to live for. The screens go black again.

"And what about pain? Do you know what pain is, boy?" he asks, and flings arms to our side, as an image appears of a car crash. A man sits inside, breathing what seems his last breaths. It's my friend. The screen goes dark.

"And what about faith, son?"he asks. But he is gone before the words stop echoing in the room.

*

The following morning I got a call from John. There was a sadness in his tone. "Will, we have to talk. Is it alright if I come over?"

"Um sure thing, John" I say.

"OK, I'll be over in a few." he says, then hangs up.

'It's a little early for John to be calling.' I think to myself. But last night I had a hell of a time sleeping, so maybe this is perfect timing. The truth is, last night, amidst my thoughts of parenthood, I realized I can't be involved in the bomber project. I also realized this may mean losing my job. But I can't spend the next few months preparing for the arrival of a life, while simultaneously building an indicator for the departure of another. It's just too grim, and too far off the end of what I deem as acceptable. It's a mindfuck, really. Even Grace agreed. She said she was going to hand off the project to one of her partners at the firm, and step back from the project for the next few months. She didn't want the stress to interfere with the pregnancy. Besides, as a full partner at her firm, she has amazing benefits. And once the baby is born, she'll decide what she wants to do from there. Truth is, she's been wanting a change for while.

We had a great talk. It's so daunting to mention some of my thoughts to her when she's so enthusiastic. But last night, we were on the same level. Filled with love for the life we were creating, and for each other. Nothing else seemed to mattered except what each of us thought. Everything else was a lesser priority. 'We work to afford the life we want, period. We don't live to work', was the mantra we agreed upon.

So I awoke this morning, both hopeful, and with a little bit of anxiety as to what I would say to John. But it was a good anxiety. An anxiety that comes with knowing you are doing the right thing. Just stand and speak. Your voice may tremble, your knees may be weak, but goodness and principle will keep your back straight. It had been a long time since I had been in this position. The last time probably being when I had met Grace, and confessed my love to her. Goodness and principle, it's a wonderful thing to have.

John arrived within a few minutes and came in and sat down. Grace was upstairs getting herself ready for her own day of delivering bittersweet news to her firm's partners. John looked down at the floor for a few moments, then spoke: "What is Central State Mental Hospital?" John asked. 'Oh. Yeah. THAT!' I thought. I tried to think of a way of telling him, in the least embarrassing way possible. But how do you tell a person you had been committed for being depressed, at the discretion of judges and psychiatrists, and still retain trust as a 'sane' human being? And how do you do it, when they think you just lied about it? The judge did rescend it from my record. "John, I'm sorry, the judge..." I said, but John cut me off. "Look Will, I know it was off your record. But these background checks, man, they are thorough. And I vouched for you..." He continued "...and they checked the records and found nothing, so it was rushed, but apparently they found a link to it somewhere." he said, his voice becoming dry. "The short of it is," he said, '...you're clearance has been revoked. I'm going to need any documents you have on the project, and I'm going to need you to sign a non-disclosure saying you won't say anything about the project to anyone." John finished. "Sure, no problem, John.' I replied, 'I don't have any documents here, they are still at the base, on my desk.' I said. 'I'm really sorry." I added. "I'm sorry too, Will.' John replied, 'This is just so stupid, I mean, it's not like you're crazy. You're a good guy. Hell, the judge even repealed the case against you. If that isn't proof of sanity I don't know what is!" John said, apologetically. "John, I'm sorry if this causes you any problems with corporate." I said. He paused, "No, they'll be fine, I'm just going to have to find another good lead engineer, that's my problem." John said, somewhat stressfully. He looked down at his shoes. Worn out brown leisure shoes that I had never seen him wear. One of the perks of the project is we don't have to be in suits. Just casual. "Well, you can go back to the home office, get back to the regular grind there. I hope this doesn't mess you and Grace up with the rental here." he said sympathetically. "Well actually John, I was going to talk with you about this today. Grace is pregnant." John looks up startled, then smiles. "So I was, actually, going to talk to you about leaving the company today, but I guess you beat me to it.' I say. 'Grace is also stepping back, so she can have less stress during the pregnancy." John is fully smiling now. "Hey Bud, that's great news. Being a parent, well... have you seen my little ones?" John says, pulls out his wallet and shows me a photo of two girls, both toddlers, both wearing dresses, standing on a beach. "We took this last year, down at Rehoboth. Aren't they something?" he says, looking fondly, the way a father does at the picture in his wallet. "Look bud, Being a parent is the most full filling thing you can do. Whatever you have to do to be there, I'm 100% behind you ."

I sign the non-disclosure form, and hand him my keys to the office. He gives me a big hug, and tells me a few more times how he supports me, and that I should call him when I'm ready to come back to the office, and if not, to call him for a recommendation for a different job in the future.

On the way out the door, John stops and says "Look bud, I know sometimes people need help. It's disgusting the way they view depression, having problems, as some kind of disease, as a stigma. They did the same kind of crap to my father after he came back from the war. 'Crazy this! Bi-polar that!'" John said, looking down. 'I think if you sat down any person with a shrink they'd conclude we're all crazy. Every single one of us. But it's just issues, it's not crazy. We've all got them, bud. I'm just sorry I had to come over here like a jerk, and tell you that you can't work on something because of it. They made me into their little henchman, made me play that part. You're a damn good engineer," John continued, "one of the best I've had, that's why I put you on my team."

I look at John and smile, "Thanks John, you're a true friend". He smiles, pats me on the shoulder, and walks out to his truck, his heavy frame shuddering with each step along the way. Looking back, he shoots a knowing smile, then ducks into the doorway of his truck, and drives off.

I close the door, and turn to see Grace coming down the stairs. "Was that John?" she asks, "What did he want?" I look at the floor, and then up to her, "Clearance issue." I say, "Central State." Her face changes to sympathy. "I love you, Will." she says, with a consoling tone. "I love you too!" I say.

Chapter 11

"Mental Health" is a relative thing. And its basis of reasoning has changed, relative to culture over the course of history. At first they thought the mentally insane were possessed by demons, relative to their god of goodness and all knowing. Then they thought we were deviations from normality, a term coined by their new god, Statistics. And over time, the treatment has changed. From treatments based on exposing us to torture and exorcism, to exposing us to electroshock and drugs. But one thing has remained the same.
We are treated as 'other'.

What I've noticed though is, the one thing us folks diagnosed with 'mental illness' have in common is that we've all been to psychologists, while those deemed as sane, have not. It's a bit of a chicken or the egg quandary, which came first, the crazy people or the people looking for crazy people, but the end result is the same. You take any teenager to a psychologist, a teenager that is experiencing the battles they feel during the socialization of teenage years, and almost all could be diagnosed with some kind of personality disorder. Emotions disorderly? Isn't that what emotions are? Isn't it the job of the brain to process emotions and filter those to which come through as action? But some folks decide it is better with the influence of a pill. And so industries have popped up to deal with us. And as society began to focus on the self, we all began to be treated by therapists, exploring the discordance between what we feel, and what has been deemed problematic for us to feel. Occasionally we find ourselves better for it. In the worst cases, we find ourselves alienated, and stigmatized. And as I learned in my time in the mental hospital, the difference between the two comes down to the doctor, whom, like yourself, is a person, and is subject to being wrong, and seeing what they want to see, based on their own personal bias. In a setting such as an asylum, or mental hospital, the staff becomes like the weather; bad staff is a storm, good staff, a sunny day.

Such was the case in my stay. The morning shift were like sunshine. But the nightshift were like storm clouds. A patient viewed as outgoing and helpful during the day, may be seen as being withdrawn, and anti-social at night. And perhaps a patient has been given a diagnoses based on this shift of patterns, with the doctor not knowing of the substantial change in treatment. But I know it's the behavior of the staff. It isn't ingrained, it's meteorological, the changing weather of the staff.

*

With Grace and I back at home, we began building space into our lives for the baby. She had taken leave, and after a few months of working from home, had adjusted to a lower-stress life. We took the room at the end our house, and changed it from being a reading room, to a nursery. It's an amazing thing; the effects of scenery on the development of a little one, so we took great care to engage the subject while exploring all possibilities. If one thing has become clear, it is our ability to fuck this kid's life up if we are not careful. And I think we will, at some level. Maybe not fuck up, but we will leave an impression. A question answered the wrong way, will affect how that little baby sees the world. We are its weather system. And so, much like how we judge a good day by if it's sunny, or a bad day by if it's rainy, if you like the rain as I do, you know that color and arrangement can play a big part towards setting mood. And some believe it can play a part towards influencing the gender of the baby.

Personally, I believe gender is set at birth, or at least set in a way that is rather solid, much like sexual preference. So the idea of gender neutrality is to not influence or re-affirm gender, but to let it develop naturally. This may save the child from the awkward moment a young boy realizes he is playing with dolls, and wonders why he is doing this if he is indeed a 'he'. Such was my own experience. But truthfully, I never really thought about it until one night I was in bed. I awoke from a dream, I'm not sure what it was about, but I do know, I awoke realizing two things: One, the strain of caretaking during the pregnancy had somewhat lopsided the emotional support in the relationship towards Grace, which was a bit odd as she usually supported me, so I needed to make a declaration that I need a little more emotional support, especially in the following point, that Two, gender wise, I'm a girl.

Just out of the blue, lying in bed, a) need more support from Grace, and b) I'm a girl. I'm a girl. "I'm a girl". Just saying it now makes me happy. I immediately jumped out of bed, and started my day on a few hours' sleep. It's 3am and I'm letting the world know that I am a girl.

But first, I did some research. 'Am I sure I'm a girl?' I asked myself. 'Let's see. Well, I do like to look at girls' clothing'. Like, if I go to a website, I check the girls section first. That makes me happy. And not to look at the girls mind you, but to look at the clothes. I only look at the men's section when I absolutely have to, and then I'm immersed in a criticism of how shitty all men's clothing looks. But a black dress; awesome. Okay, so that may be one in the 'girl' box. The second thing that occurred to me was that the majority of my best friends are girls, and my male friends are ones with not much bravado, ones that girls easily talk to. Check two in the girl box. 'But what about my masculinity?' I thought. 'What about me building things all the time? Doing stuff with my hands? Manly stuff.' Well, the latter two are gender stereotypes, women have been building things with their hands since the dawn of time. So that isn't a check in the man box, really, it's in the girl box. But what about the bravado I feel sometimes? What about my tendency to destroy physically, anything that I feel is trying to destroy me? That anger I have felt? That anger that basically destroyed my first marriage? And then it hit me… first slowly then bluntly; all of my masculine traits are protection mechanisms. I don't feel ok with my bravado at all, ever. I always feel like I'm failing to be a good human when it happens.

This blew my mind.

I had been in therapy, group therapy recently, and the majority of the folks in there talked about how they had vulnerability issues. When I'd bring up my issues, I'd generally preface it with 'I have almost the exact opposite problem!" and then talk about how I have supreme confidence in myself, and how my dilemma was in prioritizing that; in sifting through my life of things I find valuable, to try and prioritize where I should put my focus. Now I'm realizing I actually have a huge vulnerability problem. Huge! So huge I mistook it for my gender. So huge my friends argued with me that I was not, in fact, a girl and cited it as to why I was a guy.

Wow.

Realizing this, I knew the next few days would be an unravelling of what I thought to be something that was me, into something I more comfortable with. A weight was lifted off my shoulders that I didn't know was there. Feeling liberated, I began to try and map how I would handle this discovery. Would I try and pass as female? No. This is the body I have. Would it affect me sexually? No, I'm attracted to whom I'm attracted to. But maybe I'll change my name, be real about it, not hide it.

I woke Grace to tell her the news and she was excited. I could tell at first it was a shock, but she is certainly open to such things, and so immediately I felt support. After I explained my reasoning to her, my realization, I could tell she was fully behind it. Then she asked, "Will you go by 'he' or 'she'?" I hadn't thought about that, what will I go by? I do have a penis...hmm. "I'll let you know after I think about it." I said, and asked her if it would make her feel weird being married to someone that is gender-wise, a girl. She said, "I love YOU. If that's a girl, well, I fell in love with her." I smiled, and held her hand. It was a little scary, to be honest. Though it was a liberating feeling, I knew that at some point, I could be crossing societal norms in order to be me. And that can be dangerous. To someone with a family, especially one with testosterone that is pumping up from a pregnancy and becoming super protective of his baby-carrying wife, it can also be scary. Part of me wondered if it would be something I hid. The larger part of me knew I could do no such thing.

Chapter 12

Coming into the doctor's office that morning, I remembered my reaction the days after finding out Grace was pregnant. To me, it was like winning a lottery. With the lottery fantasy, you are catapulted into a world foreign to you because of the seemingly unlimited availability of something has never been unlimited; money. In this scenario, life becomes about what you can imagine. I guess that's why so many people answer the question of "What would you do if you won the lottery?" with "I'd buy a sports car." or "I'd buy a mansion." because for most of our lives, we have bought only what we could rationalize in the terms of what we could financially materialize. And so, in real life, we'd make a utilitarian choice, partly out of fear, perhaps that extravagance may cost us later down the road, which it may, and the other part, out of fear of extending ourselves, at least in the eyes of others, beyond the status we had previously lived in. We tend to regard those whom extend themselves beyond this status as irrational, irresponsible, and childish. As if being an adult means killing dreams with rationality. Grace and I do not share this idea of adulthood with our cohort. Instead, we believe adulthood to be precisely the place to build the lives we want.

To me, Parenthood was the only lottery I had ever wanted to win. Having seen my friends raise their kids, having seen parenthood as something my friends experience, and to now have that option available to me, seemed beyond my imagination. Many would fear becoming a bad parent, but I had worked through that stuff earlier. I knew if I followed my heart, if I catered to the kid, rather than tried to fit the kid into my life, I would be golden. And so, with Grace and I being the kind of people whom would be willing to make that arrangement, I had no fear. Well, I did have a fear of baby poop, and of germs. If there is one thing kids may bring, it is both of those. But I knew it would be worth it, somehow. My friends are rational people, they surely wouldn't engage in it with such joy if it wasn't worth it.

And so, sitting in this doctor's office, awaiting to see another sonogram of our baby, our little girl, I was reminded of how lucky I was. How the journey I am on now, is at the front of my imagination. Like a car driving through an unseen town, I am slowing down to see and appreciate everything. And so is Grace.

Over the next few weeks we began preparing for the birth. She had opted for a C-section as she has a small build, and her mother, of similar build, ended up the same. We had the baby shower, and amassed all the things we would need for the child. We became overrun with these things, and it took me a few weeks to move them around, and figure out how life with the baby would require us to change our lives, physically. We got a crib, and in a hurry to put order to this new life, I set it up, much to the excitement of our cats whom we would catch sleeping in it. We made the decision to let our friend adopt our more rowdy cat, as he may scratch the young baby, something I would not feel comfortable running the risk of. And soon, we found ourselves ready, and waiting, for birth.

Days were going by. Grace was getting rounder. You could see the baby kicking, which was rather startling at first, like something from a movie of aliens. And then you start to comprehend that this thing; this moving, breathing life, this heart which you have heard beating so fast and strong on the stethoscope, came from your penis, and you are at once in awe of life, and simultaneously, bewildered by the ease in which such complicated and intricate things as human beings, come to exist so easily. You look around and realize you and your partner are but two in a sea of ever re-producing humans. And suddenly you have a respect for those that came before you that you never felt before. You have a respect for this duty, a duty to the process of life itself, that before was simply academic. "I am living history!" you think to yourself, now wondering what your grandma, and great-grandma, and their grandma did with their babies in those days long ago. Suddenly you feel a continuum, of which you are part of. A process of building life. And for the first time, you see a thing you made, having a future ahead of it. A thought system. A belief system. Ethics. Love. Loss. All of which you contributed to the creation of, and shaped in how those things came to be. And you realize your current choices will be the foundation for everything else to come.

I began to research my own family, to see where we came from, how long we had been here. Perhaps I was searching for a comfort, not only of knowing my place in the continuum, but also of seeing the long productive lives of the offspring. The only fear I had was of the baby not making the term. A fear of something happening during pregnancy to complicate it. So seeing the gravestones in the family cemetery I found, actually helped. Doing the math between birth date and date of passing, I calculated "82 years, 75 years, 34 years...well he died in a war. 91 years. 54 years... Well they didn't have the technology we have now." I'd think to myself. And then I saw a small gravestone. It said, simply, "Baby Reid", and lay at the foot of the two gravestones of what I assume where it's parents. A silence came over me. And I felt a reverence for the sadness they must have felt. Standing there, I saw that cemetery as a testament to both the longevity, and fragility of life; the histories of lives passed, short and long, and that of Me, as the living product of the blood, tears, and toil of that process. Suddenly, I realized I owed my life to these people. That these people gave their lives to make my life possible. The only thing that made that palatable, was that I will to do the same for my daughter, and hopefully, my daughter for hers.

Grace wasn't really sure why we had come out to the cemetery that day. "I didn't know you cared about ancestory." she said, somewhat taken aback by my enthusiasm. "I guess it's just knowing that we're all connected, that we're making a new life," I said '...so I want to know about the old ones." I contiuned, speaking while thinking of a way to sum up what I had realized. She smiled. My dad called me on the phone, and for the first time in my life, I talked to him with a reverence for him as my father, rather than just as my dad.

Chapter 13

"The judge will see you now." the deputy said. I entered the room, this time free from shackles, perhaps they spare the judge having to view the restraints, the way the executioner is spared having to look at the faces of men put to death. "Call to order!" the deputy announced. The judge came in the room and we took our seats. I looked over to my right and saw my wife, accompanied by a friend from her work. I knew this must have been hard for her, hell, it was hard for me. But I knew what was going. For her, it must have been unbelievable, left only to her imagination of what this process would be like. To see someone she loved in the custody of the state, and so sad and defenseless. The judge questioned the institution's psychologist whom I had spoken with briefly. It was in the opinion of the psychologist, that I stay at this institution. "I believe we can help him here." the pscyhologist testified. I wondered if the psychologist had noticed my intelligence, or that I was decidedly different from the condition of the majority of his population. At this point the judge asked me a question that I would not understand the severity of, until much later. "Would you like to stay here?" he asked. Now, when a judge asks you this question, he is allowing you to make a determination, not of if you are staying here, but whether the stay will be voluntary, or involuntary. Having no one to counsel me on the true intent of the question, I answered based on what I had seen to be the condition and 'weather' of this place. "No." I answered. He then took a statement from my wife, who stated that she is at great concern for my well-being, that I had been depressed, that I had access to firearms at home, and that I had talked of suicide. I knew what was coming next. The judge began to contemplate the facts, but before he could make a judgment, I began to feel dizzy. I stood up then dropped to floor. I had passed out.

It wasn't the first time I had passed out in public, nor the last. When I have little sleep, it happens more easily. Doctors have explained it to me as a vagal response. Essentially, my intestines become upset when I have not had sleep. And when a certain threshold is reached, they exert pressure on my vagal nerve, shutting off the blood flow to my head, resulting in a loss of consciousness. You know how folks say not to push too hard while on a toilet? Same deal. This response leads to more deaths on the toilet than any other cause. And for me, well, it has resulted in many embarrassing moments. Such as the time I went to cash a check to purchase some equipment for my recording studio, and passed out at the cashier's desk, awakened to a glass of sugar water being poured into my throat, and a bank employee, placing an envelope containing a five thousand dollar deposit slip into my shirt pocket, and patting me on the chest.

But today, no check is in my pocket. Just an awakening in an ambulance, to a paramedic asking me who the president was. "President?' I muttered, 'George fucking bush." I responded angrily. The paramedic, apparently a fan of the Bush clan, responded, "...what, you don't like Bush? You some kind of leftist?" I answered, "My friend died in Iraq..." to which he responded, indignantly, "Well your friend did a good thing!" 'A good thing? Dying? Fuck you!' I thought. 'Remind me never to pass out this far south of the city ever again.' I noted to myself. And so I decided to remain silent, for fear of getting angrier.

The nurse from the state hospital, riding along with me, informed me I had been committed for a period of two weeks. Apparently it is bad form to pass out in front of a judge whom is deciding if you are able to take care of yourself on your own.

*

The morning of my daughter's birth was not much different. Barely able to sleep, my mother and I had arrived at the hospital early, eagerly awaiting what would be a life changing day. While sitting with Grace, I began to feel a little nauseous. So I wandered out to the waiting room, where I layed down on the floor. "Are you ok, you look pale!" said my wife's step-father's girlfriend. She was an EMT. I told her of my issue. She said, "There is a bathroom right over there, I'll help you to it." Somehow, over the years I had developed a habit of shitting and throwing up while engaging in the vagal response, and this was one of these times. So there I am, pants around my ankles, using the toilet, trying to puke into a trashcan she has brought over to me, while she is running from the sink and back, bringing wet paper towels to cool off my head. A few minutes later, it's done. The pressure is gone from my intestines, and I'm ready to get back to the baby game. "I need a cigarette." I say, and she helps me out to the parking lot, me feeling weak, but better than before. We talk of how excited we are about the events that will be happening this day, and I try to keep it on an academic level, for fear of arising more anxiety, and a repeat performance of fainting. I need to hold it together. I need to be able to be in the operating room. It's a sterile room so if they had any inkling I had just been shiting and puking like I had been, they'd probably ban me from attending the birth, fearing I had the flu.

I gathered my strength and began moving to the hospital door. It was going to be ok, we were going to have this baby today. We had been waiting so long, and Grace and I had already been at the hospital for a week. At the door, I went inside, and up the elevator to await the operation.

Chapter 14

I had become acquainted with the elevators of this hospital rather intimately. The week leading up to my daughter's birth were spent here riding them on smoke breaks. Grace was thirty-six weeks pregnant when she began exhibiting signs that could indicate a condition called preeclampsia. Essentially, it's protein in the urine and high blood pressure. But it can kill the baby. And it can do this without the mother knowing it. It works like this: the baby gets all of its life support through the umbilical cord, which is its sole connection to the mother, it's only life support system, much like the systems that allow an astronaut to breath while walking around outside the space ships in space. The danger in preeclampsia, is that the cord can break free from the mother, essentially cutting off the oxygen to our little astronaut. Now imagine that astronaut is not visible to anyone, and he can't cry for help, or signal that he is in distress. That is the situation the doctors were fearing, and so they admitted Grace for observation.

The first protein count in her urine was

high, but if it stayed at that rate, we would be ok. They even talked about releasing her. But after some high blood pressure readings, the second protein count came back higher. It was decided we would have to deliver early. As 37 weeks is considered full term, and we were at 36 weeks, the doctors decided to admit Grace for observation, and move the C-section from 40 weeks to 37. If anything became worse, they would order the C-section immediately. It was scary to think of our baby loosing what it needed to survive, especially so close to its birth. Grace was a mix of emotions, and my brain kicked into full support mode.

My days that week consisted of the following: Arrive at the hospital around 8 or 9 am, around the time Grace woke up, spend the day with her, and then leave around 10 or 11 at night, to go to sleep. I tried sleeping in the room the first night, but the folding chair they gave me was a bad match for my back. Grace, hating the hospital bed she was in, offered to switch with me, and that worked well, until the nurses came in for a late night check and realized the person in the bed was not their patient, but rather, her presumably able-bodied husband. Though they said it was 'OK' I couldn't help but feeling like an asshole. So I stayed at home, under the rationalization that good sleep would probably work better for her and I, as I was to handle our affairs over the next week.

And boy am I glad I did. Smoking was banned on the hospital grounds, so to smoke, I had to walk a block and a half. On top of a seven floor journey to get out of the hospital. I took the stairs the first few times, but ended up in the elevators by the end of it. I figure I went up and down those stairs about 12 times a day. My journey took me past a gift shop and a cafe, so I popped into the gift shop the first day, and bougt Grace a stuffed animal that she could hold when I wasn't there. I stopped much more frequently at the cafe for bagels for Grace and random sweets. Probably the most amazing thing about the hospital stay was the quality of food available to order in the room. Grace hadn't eaten this well in years with so little effort.

Early one morning, Grace, in a fit to quickly use the restroom, forgot to put down the jug she was supposed to pee in, and so the nurses had to throw out twenty four hours of results. Grace took this very hard, feeling like any problem with the baby now may be her fault. I had to convince her that she was doing the best anyone could hope to do. Actually, she was doing amazing. But Grace had a hard time seeing it. Someone so independent, so strong, has a hard time working with a curve ball like preeclampsia. At some level, she seemed to blame herself, for the stress, for not eating better, anything that could explain it. But I knew it wasn't her fault. Bodies do as bodies do. And I love her, so I love that body. But she couldn't see it the same, though I think she appreciated that I could.

About half way through the week, the reality of birth set in, and I realized that I had many things to get in order. She would need a breast pump, among many other things. We had been getting things ready for months, outfits for the baby, the stroller, but she had been handling most of that. I realized that, while she has the knowledge, I currently have the working feet and hands now, so it's going to be up to me to make this happen. I clicked into survival mode. I also called for the best help I could get, my mother, and began texting my best friend for advice, herself the mother of three children whom have all that they need. So between the two, I felt in good hands.

The 'hurry up and wait' attitude of the earlier part of the week soon descended into a frantic gathering of goods and supplies necessary for a smooth transition back to the house. And each night that I returned back home to sleep alone, I knew that the next time Grace came in, it would be with our Daughter. She would walk in a Mother, and I would walk in a Dad.

Chapter 15

The morning Grace and I got married was a lot like the morning she gave birth. The stars had aligned, and it was up to us to go with courage, into the path that lay in front of us. All that was required was a strength to follow our hearts, and to put our faith in the wisdom of the compass internal to each of us. We had been at the hospital the night before. It was an ER visit. Grace was having some odd symptoms, stress related probably. Between her being admitted and being seen by the doctor, we sat on the bench in the waiting room, staring into each other's eyes. We joked about how "crazy" it would be if we got married, hell, we had only known each other for 11 days. But in contemplating the 'crazy'ness, I began to wonder if it would be so crazy. We were both mature adults. Having been married before, I knew what marriage was; not a magical thing that bonds two people together, but a commitment to each other, legally, representative of the bond two people FEEL towards each other. I felt that bond towards Grace. Yes, it would be crazy to marry after only knowing each other for 11 days. But isn't that the kind of love we both would love to have? Navigating by heart, rather than by the rational? Speaking what we feel, rather than what we feel appropriate? Isn't that the love folks dream about? And isn't that indeed, the love we have?

I came back from smoking to find that Grace had been taken back to the doctor, they were ready for her. I found this out from the countless people whom had seen us sitting together. Apparently, we had been emitting an aura of love, and when people told me she had been taken back, this came through in their tone. An elderly man said "They took your wife back to be seen."
"My wife." he had called her.

I started to correct him, but his reality was what he saw. Perhaps, it was I that should correct mine. And so the next morning, sitting on her porch, surrounded by the feral cats that seemed to live there, I popped the question and she said 'yes'. She seemed to question it a little after saying yes, but not in a 'are we right for each other' kind of way, rather, in a 'am I manic', kind of way. Grace, you see, had been diagnosed with Bi-polar

Disorder earlier in life. And so she lives her life, like many folks diagnosed with Bi-Polar, questioning if her happiness is real, or mania. When I learned her conundrum, I posed the question that if she is 'just manic', then it must be me who is really insane, because I, lacking a condition that may shift my mood drastically, find it to be rationally a good idea. She laughed.

We began calling folks trying to figure out what we need to get married. An hour later, with neccessary forms in hand, we were on the Southside of town, in an elderly couple's living room; him, a justice of the peace, handing a camera to the his wife, to take pictures of us, the newly wedded couple. As Grace felt a general disdain for jewelry, and wedding rings in particular, he handed us little plastic rings that we put on each other for the ceremony,. God I love her. We spent the rest of the day trying to come up with ways to break the news to friends and family, each one becoming easier than the last.

*

The day of the birth was no different. With

courage we walked into the future. They wheeled her into the operating room first, and told me to have a seat outside. I sat there waiting. They brought me a stool to sit on. A few minutes later, they came out and took back the stool, as they needed it in the OR. I thought, 'what could they possibly need a stool for?' Minutes passed. I caught my reflection in the hallway mirror: that of a man, holding a camera, dressed in scrubs. I pleaded with myself not to pass out. Just standing there was getting to me. My nerves, and my anxiety were tremendous. And then it was time.

I walked in to find my wife looking up at me from under a sheet. They had warned me not to look, and to stay seated, as fathers tend to pass out on first sight of blood. 'Fathers.' I thought. And so I held my wife's hand, her eyes watching mine, as she lay there, open to the world, open to the life awaiting to join our family. "Family." I thought. And I began to cry. Everything we had worked towards, everything we had worked through, was coming to a head. This was it. The continuation of the continuum. The only real purpose we cannot deny in having, as humans. To bring forth life. I heard a nurse say they had a leg. I waited in anticipation. My teary eyes meeting Graces as we awaited news of more limbs. "I have an arm!" the nurse says. "Ok two limbs," I think to myself, "that's good. That's good."

I had been worried for months that the baby may be deformed, not really worried, but it had crossed my mind. News of nurses having their eyes on actual limbs began to ease this concern. "I've got a leg!" says the nurse. I began to wonder how this baby is laying in there, such that they keep getting arms and legs but not a whole baby. And before I can finish that thought, without a word from the staff, they passed by me with a baby. A purple, little, baby. Silence.

They swabbed its mouth. Still silence. I hope 37 weeks wasn't too soon. "Please cry little one." I think to myself. I pray with all my heart. And then the cry breaks the silence. The staff turns to congratulate us. "Mom" and "Dad" they say. I turn my camera to take the picture, the purple little baby, but the nurse puts her hand on top of the camera, pushing it down. "You don't want that picture. Give her a minute." I oblige and they ask

Grace if she wants to hold her. Grace nods her head, and they place our baby on Grace's chest, as they begin sewing her up. I see our daughter's little fingers. Perfect little fingers. So detailed. So delicate. I see her little nose. Her little mouth. She is nothing like I had expected. She is better than I could have imagined. A little life. Our little daughter. Our little family. I look at Grace, and she looks at me. We smile.

Chapter 16

Few times in life are you as sure of doing the right thing, as you are after birth. Nothing can come close to it. It's an amazing feeling. But birth rearranges your life back around the little one you have brought life to. So in the following weeks, you begin to incorporate yourself, your old worn tendencies, into the new life you will live. Accordingly, birth can be as much of a new life for the parents as it is for their baby. And yet for some parents, it only adds obligation. Grace and I were of the former. And so we began to work out the angles of our new life.

I, for one, was sick of our car, and so was Grace. It's amazing how even the biggest car can seem so small, once packed with the supplies required of a baby. Road trips to see family had become a game of Tetris, but with something always left behind. "Do we want to bring the crib, or the stroller?" we'd ask ourselves. Obviously, we'd need the crib, so vacations became occasions where we were limited to short walking distances. 'Time to find something new.' we realized. "How about something big, something with space?" we wondered. And soon we find ourselves trading in our two-door coupe for a family car. A Buick. And the only thing I found insane about it, is how awesome I found that Buick to be. A Buick for christsake!

And then there is the house. What seemed to be fun and perfect for us began to seem like a series of booby traps to a child, and the separation afforded by the stairs becomes a nuisance when the baby is on a different floor.

And so we began to become slightly different people. In traffic, the idiot in front of us driving fifteen miles-per-hour in a zone designated as twenty-five, soon becomes a possibly distracted parent that we empathize with. And the cute little outfits we had hoped to get her soon become whatever we find at the thrifstore or in hand-me-downs from friends and family, because she will grow out of it in a few months. And soon we find ourselves as less judgmental people, and an entire part of the world that we just couldn't understand a few months before, begins to make perfect sense. My younger self may have accused this transformation as that of 'selling out'. But I'd make a distinction. 'Selling Out' to me, will never come from cultivating understanding or compassion for those around us, but rather, for ignoring understanding and the impulses of our heart in an attempt to find a life that simply meets a minimal set of standards, a lowball set of demands of what we want from life. Deconstructing love to find a flaw is selling out. Being angry at someone for not meeting the requirements of time and money you have in your head, is selling out. Forgetting about love, and suffering, and the beauty and the tragedy of life, in order to live more comfortably, is selling out. But embracing life, as you know it to be true, is the opposite of selling out. It is the strengthening of our hearts, the root of all passion.

*

It had been about seven months since our daughters birth when my friend, the existential crisis, came back to visit me. But this time, he had a different face. Whereas before, I had wondered about where I placed my value, hunting between the various things I could invest my time in, to try and make life a little easier, a little more purposeful. But now, I had purpose. The problem I faced this time was; is there anything I can do that seems as remotely important as my newborn daughter? If it's down to writing a song, or washing her bottles, the bottles always win. If it's down to having a day doing anything I used to do, or spending the day reading with her, the reading always wins. Nothing else compares. I suppose this is the life of the parent, yet it is not without complete reward. The struggle becomes, how to incorporate those things I do, the things that made me who I am, back into my life? Or, do I need to incorporate them at all? This is where the crisis centers. A respect for the life you had, and not wanting to simply throw it away, balanced with a realization that nothing compares to your child.

But without realizing it, life tends to balance out. You catch yourself painting while the baby is sleeping. You catch yourself taking photos while out on a walk with her. You think up lyrics while changing her diaper, and you realize you couldn't suppress the real you, even if you tried. All you can do is ignore it, and even that is futile.

The moment of change for me, came with the understanding that I don't have to work at who I am, but only who I want to be. And who I am, is pretty damn good right now. And with that, the stress, for the most part, went away. The antithesis to this is the self of a nineteen year old, the person searching to build identity in everything they can. The person searching for meaning in every statement they make, and vehemently defending even the simplest of words when they are questioned. But its not the words they are defending, its the identity behind it. And so when I look to my life, to question whether I am focusing on something too hard, staking identity in a thing rather than sheer love of the activity, ideal, or belief; I use my imaginary nineteen year old self as litmus test.

Chapter 17

The hardest part of being an abusive asshole, is admitting it to yourself, without losing the strength to overcome it. Most abusive people seem to admit such facts to themselves, only to use the realization as confirmation, or rationalization, for continuing to act shitty. Much like no one worries about the way furniture is arranged in a house that is on fire, I, being abusive, just tended to accept that being violent was who I was. The real question was 'Why is my wife still with me?'

The days ending my first marriage were the days of me in the mental hospital. It was a marriage that had started out amazing, but, in hindsight, was too mature for me. I realize now that I had too many issues, and too many unaddressed fears and vulnerabilities, to really be able to participate in a healthy relationship. And this was most obvious in the times I hit my wife, and in the frequent name calling. It's almost as if I hated her for being able to love me. Because, deep down, I hated myself. It was a situation such a world away from where I would be ten years later, and such a world away from being the person that Grace could fall in love with.

It took a lot of work to overcome violence being a solution to vulnerability in my life. It took many years of therapy, and many years of loneliness; sometimes out of fear of being violent again, and sometimes out of sheer depression from how I had been before. And for each day of loneliness I felt, it was something of a movement towards a better world, of shielding me and my abuse from the world. But this was a cop-out, and a self-martyring one at that. And having been the one that had acted abusive, I was a long way away from deserving any kind of respect for any further actions until I confronted abuse head on, and actually put in the work to be a good person to others, esepecially the one's I love.

The day my wife testified in court against me was the day I realized how she, now protecting herself from me, needed to operate. And seeing her there in that way, I knew I needed to do my part and get right with myself and the people around me.

Statistically, I probably became physically

and verbally abusive because I was abused as a kid. That seems to be the way it works. Something about being in an abusive situation seems to make it easier to become abusive towards others. Over the years, I've come to think it's because of the suppression of feelings one gets used to in being abused, coupled with a vulnerability from anticipating violence. So one ends up feeling very vulnerable, fearing the worst, and acting out in a violent manner, more violent than they probably would have if they were not suppressing their feelings so much.

So my road to overcoming these behaviors focused on being present with what I was feeling: Am I vulnerable? Yes. Is that Ok? Yes. Do I really want to treat my partner this way? No. Some simple questions like this, if applied in that relationship, would have most likely resulted in very different outcomes. But unfortunately, I was too selfish, and too self-immersed in my own situations, to pay attention to the reality of how my actions affected her.

The scariest thing, was that I did not even realize I was an 'abuser' until we split up. I knew I had hit my wife. But I always thought it was because I was angry, or because I lost control. I could not see the bigger picture. It took me reading a list of abusive behaviors that I had found on the internet, for it to finally click. And when it did click, I was destroyed. Having grown up seeing the same shit happen to people I loved, to know I had done almost the exact same thing, brought me to a devastating level of understanding.

And so that was my motivation to overcome abusive behavior. And it required rethinking how I look at the entire world. People don't 'make' me angry; but rather, I get angry. In fact, people don't 'make' me do anything, I react that way. And my actions, they were not something in my genes from family, but in fact a decision I was making; I was choosing to be violent. That may seem kind of obvious to some folks, but it did not seem obvious to me. I thought that I was violent inherently, like those violent before me, and that anyone in a relationship with me, would have to understand that. And instead of not thinking of hitting someone, it would be something I would have to work to 'manage'. I thought the feeling of violence was natural, but that most folks just didn't do it, and I was just weak. It wasn't until after a few therapy sessions that it clicked with me; that it's not just a problem of self-control, but an entire problem of the way I view and relate myself to others.

Once I had that point in mind, that I knew I was accountable for every action, every word, that no one 'made' me, or caused me to do anything, and that it was up to me to treat others the way I ideally want to treat them, instead of just reacting to anger, and floundering to my emotions and vulnerabilities; once I had realized all that, it was then that I had a solid basis to change. Moving forward required me to rebuild my life from one where I expected violence, a hold-over from growing up with abuse, to life where it wasn't an option. So, gone were the guns I had acquired to protect myself from the world. Gone were the songs I'd listen to that seemed to re-enforce the idea that the world is a place to defend yourself from. And gone was the view that everyone may hurt you. 'Some people may hurt me, but they are few and far between.' I'd tell myself. And in place of all these things, I put a view of compassion for other beings. I read a lot of Buddhism, and discovered that I truly believed that people all start out as good, it's just how we understand and deal with the world that shakes us from that path. That lead me to a compassion for all people, and for myself.

When I met Grace, I had been on this path of self-correction and self-understanding for six years. And I am so glad for it.

*

It's hard to imagine that a person such as Grace; so strong, so funny, so optimistic, could have been in a situation where she was abused, but she had been in some unfortunate relationships before she met me. In fact, her first two boyfriends were abusive both physically and verbally. And being the caring person she is, had found herself using that caring, those positive qualities, to almost rationalize the shitty way those guys had treated her.

She shared this with me the first day we met, and it really blew my mind. 'Really?' I had asked her. "Yes." she said. I then told her my story of how I had been abusive to my ex-wife. She paused for a moment, taking it in, and then said, in a tone I never heard her take ever again 'I won't be abused.' then, turning to a look of understanding said '...but I don't think that's who you are anymore.' That statement blew my mind. Here we were, two folks that had been abused, and me having been abusive as well, and she was making this judgment, so quick into meeting me. I knew I wasn't like that anymore, I knew that in the relationships following my ex-wife, the biggest complaints my ex's probably have about me would be that I was disconnected sometimes, depressed, or aloof, or maybe that I pushed them away a little, but nothing like abuse, or my past. It was a very compassionate thing. And I think it helped to form a bond of trust in some way, almost immediately between her and I. Talking of abuse seems taboo, especially in abusive relationships; abusers and the abused rarely talk about it. So having this statement flat out, between two folks, at the beginning of the relationship, that it would be unacceptable, really set a tone, that for once, I felt comfortable in.

In past relationships, when telling exes of my abusive past, it almost seemed like my exes dismissed it, not like they were ok with it, but that they just did not want to think of it. And in that, it was as if they could not accept that abuse had been a reality of my life. In doing this, I don't think they could understand what it was like for me to be there with them presently. No matter how much I despised my abusive actions of the past, I had to accept that I had done that, and many of the best things in me, like patience, came from working through them.

With Grace, it seemed like what I had worked through, had been noted, accepted, and that it was understood, that we were two people, whom had been through some horrible shit, trusting each other not to hurt the other. Willing to see if she could trust a person again, if I could trust a person again, and if I could honor that trust without violating it.

And I have to admit, it scared me. It put a pressure on me. To be the person I knew I could be, and deep inside, was. It was almost like a test.

But one that would go on as continually as I would know Grace. But it was a test of something I knew I could do, and at this point, pretty easily. I guess the closest analogy I can think of is for someone to grade you on stating your name. You know your name, but being put on the spot like that, was a little scary. But I realized that is how it SHOULD be. All I knew was, if I was going to ever have a healthy, rewarding relationship, while being the person I wanted to be; this relationship with Grace was the time to have it.

And so that night, the night of the first day I met Grace, holding hands, talking of our pasts and what we wanted from the future, it felt like both a graduation from the past, and the birth of a new life that each of us had known was theoretically possible, but we were now living. It was quite possibly the most amazing thing I have ever felt.

Chapter 18

My wife had picked me up that Monday afternoon from the mental hospital. As I had been brought in on a Friday evening, Monday was the first day I had been able to see the psychologist. After being committed, they had transferred me from the state hospital to a more appropriate clinic. One with patients I could identify with, instead of just feeling sorrow for. The most helpful was our group sessions where I met people with bi-polar, schizophrenia, some with both bi-polar and schizophrenia, and some that had PSTD. Many, I learned were there by choice, and they came when they knew they needed to. A few of the men called me the 'mad professor', because, with my shaggy hair, and intellect, I was something like a professor to them, and mad, well, because I was their cohort.

The psychologist told me it sounded like a general depression, and between my health and the dissolving relationship between me and my wife, that my depression seemed more situational than chemical. And so I was free to go.

Upon arrival of my wife, my fellow patients

remarked how beautiful she was, and how lucky I was to have her. It was bittersweet, as for a while she was indeed in my life, but we both knew now, it was best for us to go our separate ways. We were able to remain friends after the divorce, but I would feel shame for how I treated her. I apologized a few times. Apologies are good for the soul.

The next few years I spent mostly alone. I felt horrible about my past abuse to her, and where healthy folks may have gone out and built a new relationship, I spent the time reflecting on my past actions, both in therapy, and with myself. I did not want to treat anyone the way I had treated her, ever again. When my health, or depression, or loneliness would grind me down, I used a motivational trick to keep me in good spirits: I imagined a house, and at the window of that house was a young child looking out the window. His mother would come to the window, and ask 'What are you looking at?" The child would reply, "I'm waiting for daddy." His mother would smile, and then, look out the window herself, waiting for her husband to come home. Outside that window it was raining. And outside that scenario was me, I was the father, I was the husband. And it was my job to make sure that one day, I could walk through that door, and fulfill the meaning those two people held in me. That was my goal; to arrive at that house one day, and be able to love them, and to love myself, and treat the people in my life with love and compassion; the way they deserved to be treated.

*

A few months after our daughter's birth, I was sitting with Grace on the couch, and realized, it had been a while since I had been depressed. And then I remembered my coping device, the one of the child and wife, waiting for me to come home. I looked at our daughter, her smiling at me with the big grin she elicits from morning 'till night. I am her daddy. And then I looked at my wife, and she looked at me with that loving look she gives me. I am her husband. And I realized:
'I'm here. Girls, I'm home. I love you both.'

www.ingramcontent.com/pod-product-compliance
Lightning Source LLC
Chambersburg PA
CBHW070329120726
47909CB00008B/2663